Praise for *BEEP!*

BEEP!
Navigating Through ADHD

WRITTEN AND ILLUSTRATED BY
GARRETT RITCHIE

WITH 4114U ILLUSTRATIONS BY JULIA PAUL-FISHER

Dedications:

This book is dedicated to my mother, my father, my brother, my publisher, my 6th grade teacher, my cat, my laptop, that guy who picked up my pencil for me that one time, and most of all, myself.
—Garrett Ritchie

I would like to dedicate this book to my husband and two boys who continue to inspire and motivate me. May I continue to share that energy of love and enthusiasm to every child I teach.
—Carey Averill, M.Ed.

I would like to dedicate this book to my wonderful family for the unconditional love they give me as I seek to support my students with special needs.
—Susan Van Zanten, M.A.Ed.

Charity:
A portion of sales from this book will be donated to Just in Time Foster Youth
www.jitfosteryouth.org

Sales:
The student author and illustrator of this book will be distributing a portion of their earnings into their college savings funds.

REFLECTIONS
PUBLISHING

4114U: How to Read and Use This Book

Dear Reader,

You may be reading this story for pleasure, or you may have chosen this book because you can relate to its subject matter. Either way, here are some helpful instructions to navigate and guide your way through this book:

1. Read and enjoy the story and notice the vocabulary footnotes; remember the story was written and illustrated by kids just like you. If you feel like you are having trouble focusing on your schoolwork or daily tasks, then ask yourself if you can relate to the main character in this story.

2. After you read the story, you will find a section called 4114U. This section has been put together by experts to give you some helpful tips and advice on how to work through these feelings of anxiety. You will find activities to do by yourself along with some helpful activities to do with a parent or loved one.

Because true healing requires you to focus on your emotional, educational, social, and even spiritual needs, we have divided the 4114U portion of the book into the following three sections:

• Action Steps to Help Families Emotionally
• Action Steps to Help Families Socially
• Action Steps to Help Families Spiritually and Holistically

One of our goals is for you to feel like this book was written just for you; we want you to see that many other people struggle with ADHD and you are not alone. We also want to give you some hope that things will get better, and to empower you (and your parents) by providing the necessary tools needed to deal with overcoming your ADHD.

While we hope you will find this book helpful, please keep in mind that its content is not intended to be a substitute for any professional medical advice, diagnosis, or treatment. We hope you enjoy this book.

All the best,

Colleen C. Oster

President/Publisher, Reflections Publishing

Acknowledgements:

A wise elementary principal once told me that our job as parents and educators is to teach our children the coping tools they need. By preparing children for challenging experiences like getting bullied, merging new and old friends, and developing life long study skills, they will hopefully have the tips and tools they need in their back pockets to pull out and utilize when necessary.

This is the mission of Reflections Publishing —to allow children to help their peers through the power of their stories and illustrations, and to allow experts to equip kids with the tools needed to thrive in today's world.

This book would not have been possible without the numerous brainstorming and editing sessions with the following people. I thank you for your many hours of dedication and passion to this mission.

Colleen C. Ster
President/Publisher of Reflections Publishing

Educators: Carey Averill, Lindsey Bullis, Kim Duba, Erica Rood, Kristin Soderberg, and Susan VanZanten

Business Professionals: Kelley Carlson, Autumn Chandler, Jessie Colburn, and Heather Roth

Child Psychologists/Family Therapists/Medical Doctors: Renee DiToro, ACC, CPCC; Donica Dohrenwend, Ph.D.; Dr. Doug Nguyen, M.D., and Lewis Ribner, Ph.D.

Student Editorial Team: Julia Paul-Fisher, Cole Chandler, Madison Chandler, Alex Ster, Caroline Ster, and Isabelle Ster

REFLECTIONS
PUBLISHING

Table of Contents

4114U Section

Published by Reflections Publishing
© 2016 Reflections Publishing.

This book is a work of fiction. Names, characters, businesses, organizations, places, events, and incidents either are the product of the author's imagination or are used fictitiously. Any resemblance to actual persons, living or dead, events, or locales is entirely coincidental.

First Edition. Published in the United States of America.

ISBN 978-1-61660-013-6

Visit our website at www.reflectionspublishing.com for more information or inquiries.

"To tell a person who has ADD to try harder is about as helpful as telling someone who is nearsighted to squint harder."

"People with ADD often have a special 'feel' for life, a way of seeing right into the heart of matters, while others have to reason their way along methodically."
- Edward M. Hallowell, *Delivered from Distraction*

Chapter 1:
Beep! Beep!

"Beep…Beep…Beep!" The alarm droned, but 11-year-old Jack Winthrop wasn't surprised. Typically, when someone is surprised by an alarm clock, it is usually because their sleep has been interrupted. Unfortunately for Jack, there was nothing to interrupt, because there had been no sleep. Kids often would ask him why he looked so tired or why he had bags under his eyes.

Jack would often think, *if they had ADHD [1] (Attention Deficit Hyperactivity Disorder) like I do they would know.*

Although the annoying sound of the alarm clock could be put to rest by the simple press of a button, Jack knew that the irritating sound would linger throughout his whole day. He got up and pressed the button to stop the beeping sound. It was dead for now.

After this came the dreaded trek downstairs into the food pit—otherwise known as the kitchen. It was here that he heard the second alarm clock—his mother. While most kids enjoy chocolate flavored breakfast cereals or have cereals filled with marshmallows, the "Mom Clock" would only allow him to eat a special cereal, which Jack thought tasted like paper. The bland flavor replaced the chocolate flavor, and instead of marshmallows, there were dark red and wrinkly fruits in the cereal that had a very distinct, dried grape flavor. The reason Jack connected the taste of cereal to paper was because the cereal was called Book-O's. It claimed to make children focus better at school because it contained some sort of brain herb found in certain species of trees. Of course, one of the few things Jack knew for sure was that paper came from trees. As for the effectiveness of the cereal, the only book that Jack was familiar with was the one he felt inside of him after he forced down a bowl. As soon as

[1] ADHD (Attention Deficit Hyperactivity Disorder): Affects around 5% of children in the U.S. It is one of the most common childhood disorders.

he swallowed the last bite, his mom encouraged him to go get ready for school.

Jack emerged from the food pit and climbed up what felt like Mount Everest. As he walked up the staircase, he looked out the window and saw something move out of the corner of his eye.

Rabbit! There's a rabbit outside!

Completely forgetting that he was supposed to be getting dressed for school, Jack pressed his face against the window and was reminded of a story he had read. It was about a Native American legend, and one of the few stories he had ever read. The legend stated that if you stare at an animal long enough and recite a certain chant, you can hear what the animal is thinking. So Jack did just that, but for some strange reason, the rabbit kept chanting over and over, "Get upstairs! How are you still walking up the STAIRS?!" Jack soon discovered that the sound was coming from the alarm clock in the food pit… his "Mom Clock." He once tried to find the "off" button for the "Mom Clock," but quickly learned that was a bad idea.

When Jack returned to home base, a.k.a. his room, he peered into his eclectic[2] wardrobe housed in what some creatures referred to as "The Closet of Knowledge." Okay, he made up the knowledge part, but Jack found a lot of things boring and would often make up things in his head to make his life more interesting.

[2] eclectic: a wide range of different styles

He had a theory that when he was a very young boy, he was accidentally locked in a closet and stayed there for about two hours. Ever since then, he had an extreme dislike of closets, and so "The Closet of Knowledge" was born. One of the things that he really didn't like about closets is that, for some reason, whenever he entered one, he felt compelled to put on clothes. Not to mention that choosing what to wear would be a challenge. (Of course, one benefit of looking into a closet and needing to find something to wear is that there are endless possibilities. A person can choose any combination, and it's not as boring as having to wear a school uniform.)

There was another reason that Jack didn't like closets. He once saw a movie in which a girl stepped into a closet and entered another world. One time, Jack tried to search for that same magical portal,[3] and he did, in fact, find a door. When he opened the door, he found a land full of wonderful colors and rainbows. It was so real that Jack imagined he could reach out and touch it. But when he actually stuck his hand into the closet, he felt the electrical network of wires, and one of the broken wires shocked him and pulled him back to reality.

His dad said that everyone shocks themselves at least once in their lifetime. Now, looking back, Jack remembered how his father didn't say that everyone did that eight more times. These eight other times may have been when he got locked in "The Closet … of Wisdom… or Knowledge… or Triumph. The

[3] portal: an entrance to a tunnel

Closet of Tri—"

I forgot to brush my teeth!

So Jack ran into the bathroom and picked up
his electric toothbrush. It worked very simply: After
the switch is flipped, it vibrates and releases a pulsar[4]
beam that destroys anything in its path. ZAP KOW!
ZAP POW!

I'm still in my pajamas!

Jack rushed into the closet, and when he emerged,
he was wearing a heavy, fully operational set of armor.
He watched his enemies throw spears and shoot laser
rays at him so that they could wound him. But ALL
IN VAIN—

I still haven't brushed my teeth!

[4] pulsar: rotate very rapidly and emit very regular pulses of polarized
radiation (dictionary.com)

Chapter 2:
So it Begins

When Jack was done scrubbing his pearly whites, it was time to go to the Prison of Nadeed, otherwise known as school. He rushed downstairs, ran outside

[5] transporter: an object that carries or moves someone from one place to another.

and hopped in the yellow "transporter"[5] that would take him to the prison, a.k.a. school.

On the bus, there was another very loud alarm clock. His name was Lenny. Lenny had blonde hair, blue eyes, and a thick, football player-type build. Although very athletic, he was not known for being the "sharpest tool in the shed." He was also known as a bully. Not only did he bully Jack in P.E. class, he was also right by Jack's side in his worst subject— English. Lenny noticed every flaw, every weird thing about Jack—his sleepless, sunken eyes, untied shoelaces, hair that he always forgot to brush—and Lenny had to announce everything. While Jack would frequently find himself embarrassed, the reality was that Lenny enjoyed diverting[6] attention to his victim, so others wouldn't ridicule[7] him for his lack of intelligence.

Luckily today, there was an open seat next to Nicholas Fent; his nickname was Smiley. Smiley and Jack had been friends since fifth grade. They met each other at Jack's child psychologist's[8] office while Jack waited to be called in for his ADHD evaluation appointment. Smiley was there because he had come straight from school with his mom for his older brother's appointment.

Jack was there to be evaluated because he had trouble focusing, sitting still, and paying attention in

---

[6] diverting: to direct attention towards something from something else.

[7] ridicule: make fun of, tease, or mock

[8] pyschologist: A person that specializes in diagnosing ADHD and treating individuals when they feel they are experiencing an emotional distiburbance or dissapointment in their life.

class. His mom was concerned because she saw his grades dropping and that he was developing test anxiety.[9] Jack often ran into Smiley at the doctor's office because both of their moms would make appointments right after school. Much to Jack's chagrin,[10] he learned that he had to go to appointments on a regular basis to have his blood pressure monitored and to be weighed. A couple of the medicines that are prescribed to help manage the symptoms of ADHD like Adderall®, Vyvanse®, and Concerta® can cause some kids to lose weight because the medications can decrease appetite and make you a bit nausea.

Jack and Smiley met one day when Jack's doctor was running behind schedule. Jack was reading his comic book while he waited. Being a comic book fan, Smiley noticed the comic book cover and struck up a conversation with Jack. They discovered that even though they went to different elementary schools, they were actually only a five-minute bike ride away from each other. They also learned they had a lot in common and decided to exchange cell phone numbers so they could start swapping comic books.

When Jack's doctor called him in, he handed the comic book to Smiley and said, "Keep it." Since then, they've been buds for life.

* * *

Flash forward to when it was time to go to middle school, and Jack was excited to leave his small, familiar campus and go to Carmel Valley Middle School with Smiley. He was especially relieved because Smiley

[9] anxiety: to have nervous behavior, uneasiness, to be filled with worry
[10] chagrin: disappointment

would be there to protect Jack from Lenny. Smiley was big like Lenny, but taller and more muscular. Most people believed that Smiley was the person whom Lenny was most afraid of, but Jack knew that was not true. Smiley was a close second. The person Lenny was most afraid of was Jack's younger sister, 6-year- old, Madeline. The reason Lenny was afraid of her was the same reason why Jack's family would know if she was ever kidnapped. They would know because Madeline was so sassy and mean, the kidnappers would give her back! She had a piercing, constant scream, nails that left scars, and would bite to draw blood.

Madeline was very cute, but still very dangerous. For example, Jack's 9-year-old brother, Nate, was always pulling nasty pranks on Lenny. Many times when he embarked on these endeavors,[11] Nate was accompanied by his trusty sidekick, Madeline. Nate was always the brains of the operation, and Madeline was there to help execute the plan. Madeline was effective because she had no fear. Together, they could pull off the worst of pranks, and Lenny was their most frequent victim.

Jack remembered the last prank she pulled, and wondered if Lenny was ever going to be able to pull the hair bands off his wisdom teeth. Jack didn't like to talk about what he remembered from that day. It was just...gross.

* * *

[11] endeavors: to try hard; to put effort into something

As they drove on the bus, Lenny did not say anything because he knew that if he did, Smiley would make it so he wouldn't say another word.

"I'm telling you, Jack," said Smiley, "the secret to a terrorist-free flight is shrink-raids."

Jack looked puzzled. "Please enlighten me, my dear friend."

So Smiley explained, "If the government shrinks passengers and all of their belongings before they get on the plane, and the entire flight crew remains normal size, then not only would it create more space for more passengers, it would also render any terrorism attempt to be futile." [12]

As Smiley talked, Jack focused on the little bumps on the surface of his backpack. He imagined what it would be like if there were tiny people who lived on his backpack, and the little bumps would be like mountains. The people would climb these "mountains," and Jack's entire life with his backpack would influence the weather and geographic occurrences in this little tiny world. He could hear what sounded like chanting in the heavens of this new world, which got louder and clearer until he realized that he was still in a conversation with Smiley.

When Jack awoke from his daydream, the transporter had finally arrived at the Prison of Nadeed. This was where the torture began. Because they had different classes, Smiley was no longer there to protect Jack. But Lenny was there. Lenny, like any good "friend," was always hanging out with Jack in the "very

---

[12] futile: useless

educational and very intelligent" physical education class. Today they played dodgeball and, of course, Lenny was on the opposite team. Usually, when a player hits someone with a headshot in P.E., they get disqualified and can't play anymore. But Lenny decided that for Jack, it was totally worth it. It can be assumed what happened next...

If you guessed that Lenny hurled a ball at Jack's head then you would be correct. As Jack felt the ball smack his head, he felt the room start spinning and thought he was going to pass out. As he started to regain his vision, he could see Lenny laughing and pointing at him.

Thankfully, P.E. class was finally over and next came Art Class. This was also challenging for Jack because Jack was color-blind. Jack could see colors, but he would get certain colors confused with others. In Jack's case, it was usually brown and red, but sometimes it was green and yellow, and other times orange and yellow.

Once he was drawing what he intended to be a brown bear, and his teacher said, "Oh, what a beautiful red rat!" Of course, laughter ensued.[13] From that point forward, Jack refused to color any pictures publicly and limited his artwork to his doodles.

[13] ensued: followed, came afterward

Chapter 3:
Ms. Stiche Has a Really Big Nose!

The class Jack most dreaded, though, was English. He was comfortable with Math, History, Science, and Multimedia, but not English. For Jack, English class was mostly staring at words. He just couldn't handle it! He was often caught staring into space, which was strange because staring into space usually would seem extremely boring. But no, he did more staring into space than writing in English. Of course, Lenny, was always a "good" buddy and reminded Jack that he was daydreaming and made sure the whole class knew about it.

There was another alarm clock in that class and her name was Ms. Stiche—at least, Jack thought it was a she. She claimed her first name was Verna, but something in Jack's gut told him that her real name was Dennis. Ms. Stiche made it clear to Jack that she didn't believe in ADHD. She thought it was just an excuse that doctors made up for hyperactive kids so that they could get out of schoolwork. This only increased Jack's angst[14] when she was present.

As Jack looked up at Ms. Stiche, he noticed her gigantic dorsal[15] fin-shaped nose, and her curly, stringy hair that had been dyed brown. If someone looked closely at her, though, they could tell that it was actually gray. They could see the dye marks from where she spray-painted herself on her forehead. Ms. Stiche was also tall and lanky.[16] She liked to be viewed as upper class—a prestigious[17] middle school English teacher. She pointed her elongated[18] fingernail at Jack's nose, perhaps thinking to herself... *if only I had a normal-sized nose like that.*

Jack had watched a television show about spies and learned that someone could tell if a person was female if their ring finger was longer than their index finger. One time, Jack tested this theory on Ms. Stiche while she was taking one of her regular, mid-class naps. She woke up almost immediately after he started

[14] angst: anxiety, dreadful feeling

[15] dorsal: situated on or toward the upper side of the body (dictionary.com)

[16] lanky: thin and bony

[17] prestigious: exceptional reputation, highly thought of

[18] elongated: extremely long, extended

investigating. But in that short half-second, Jack could have sworn her index finger was longer than her ring finger.

Right now, the nail of her index finger looked like it was about to slice his nose open, perhaps so she could surgically replace her large nose with his. She told Jack, "Beep-Beep-Beep-Beep-Beep-Beep!" which almost sounded like, "Get to work, Mr. Jack, or it's another detention for you!"

Ms. Stiche has a really big nose.

Jack tried his hardest to make sounds in his head to match what the words on the page said. Unfortunately, he often found himself drifting off to a familiar place where he found himself in a battle fighting giant ogres and using a club to bash the brains of the Sorcerer of Jocra. The Sorcerer of Jocra didn't appreciate having her head rapped by a ruler.

Ms. Stiche has a really big nose.

Jack was snapped sharply out of his daydream when Ms. Stiche barked, "Double detention for three weeks!" That was his sentence.

The only good thing about English class was Miss Robertson, the student teacher for Ms. Stiche. For some reason, Miss Robertson was very nice to Jack, and Jack was quite certain she was a girl. Miss Robertson was very patient with Jack and didn't seem to have the same "sight problems" when Lenny was bullying Jack. (Ms. Stiche often overlooked Lenny's bullying. It was probably because she thought Jack deserved it.)

Jack knew that Miss Robertson didn't exactly like Lenny. Her motto was: treat others the way you would want to be treated, unless it's Lenny, then do what you need to do." Okay, she wouldn't really say the part about Lenny, but it was implied. Jack knew that Miss Robertson was always watching Lenny and, in the end, looking out for Jack.

Ms. Stiche has a really big nose. Jack simply could not ignore it—no matter how hard he tried.

Miss Robertson leaned over to Jack and said, "I'll make sure I get to the school database[19] and get you out of that detention."

Jack asked, "Why are you doing all of this stuff for me?"

She replied: "Well, you and I are a lot alike. I have ADHD, too and I understand what you're going through."

Jack asked, "Then why don't you just tell Ms. Stiche that?"

"If I told Ms. Stiche that I have ADHD, I wouldn't be helping you in this classroom anymore."

Ms. Stiche has a really big nose.

---

[19] database: collection of data in a computer

Chapter 4:
Challenge Accepted

The one thing that Jack actually looked forward to during his school day was lunch time. He ate lunch at a table in front of the library, next to Smiley. As Jack looked through his lunch, he investigated what kind of cruel and unusual punishment the motherboard alarm clock had packed for him. One of the things in his lunch box was some sort of sandwich —or maybe it was a bagel or worse, a bunch of candle wax. Whatever it was, it looked like it had just come from a portable toilet for squids, and it smelled like feet! Jack would much rather eat Book-O's mashed together with turnips than *this*.

Jack thought, I can skip lunch for one day, can't I? It was a strategy that Jack had been using for every lunch ever since he started school. Jack knew that his mother would not enjoy this, so, as he did every day, he disposed of the evidence by dumping all of the contents of his lunch box into the trash can. It still amazed Jack that his mother never asked what happened to all of those ice packs.

Jack compared his lunch to Smiley's, which looked as if it could have been prepared by Willy Wonka himself. It was a big mistake to look at Smiley's lunch, because after he did, he couldn't stop staring. He didn't need to stare for long, though, because after a few seconds, it was gone. Actually, it wasn't really gone. Jack had learned about the law of conservation of mass in science class. Mass is never destroyed or created during a chemical reaction. In this case, the chemical reaction was Smiley's digestion. Jack knew that either way, Smiley's lunch wasn't coming back.

After the daring adventurers' hearty meal was over, they headed into the library to read comic books. Smiley started to carry on about how he and Jack could have their own segment on the Carmel Valley Middle School's student broadcast.

"Yeah! I thought we could have something like a prank show," Smiley said. "We could get hidden cameras and hide, and then some unsuspecting fool would get pranked. Then we'd jump out and yell, 'You just got ripped!'"

"You just got ripped?" said Jack, disappointed in Smiley's.

"Yeah! You know, like Jack the Ripper, because your name is Jack."

"Right Smiley, because that is the person I most want people to associate me with," while shaking his head no.

In the library, Jack noticed all the kids reading real books, not comic books like he read, but books that actually had words all the way through. He was amazed at how they kept reading, and reading, and reading, and they didn't fall asleep or anything! Jack couldn't stare at a bunch of black squiggles for that long. Watching the other kids in the library made Jack certain he wasn't normal. Analyzing his fellow students, Jack felt like a lost soul. When he observed his fellow classmates reading, he felt like a therapist, or what he thought a therapist must feel like as they sit back and watch and analyze others.

Snap out of it!

Jack took a breath and collected himself. This was it, he thought, the moment of truth. In order to impress his friend and his family, and his teacher, and his classmates, and himself, Jack—right then and there—knew that he must successfully read a book. Not just any book—he needed to read a really thick book. Maybe even multiple books!

Challenge considered, he thought.

Then Lenny passed him and said: "Yeah, Winthrop! Why don't you check out a reading machine?"

In that moment, Jack decided: Challenge accepted.

He journeyed through all of the library's sections—Biographies, Historical Fiction, Fantasy—none of the books he saw appealed to him until he got to the Science Fiction center. He looked around at all of the socially awkward, buck-toothed, braces-wearing nerds with glasses that were about an inch thick, who enjoyed role-playing games and talking about fan fiction. The first thing Jack did was question his own interest in the book Ultra Wars. This was a Sci-fi book series he had started and stopped reading many times. He decided that he might as well deny the book challenge he had given to himself.

But then he saw it.

He saw something that mysteriously compelled[20] him forward. He removed the book from the shelf and found out it was a series of short stories by Ray Bradbury. The book was titled The Machineries of Joy and was about an inch thick. At first, it looked really long and boring, but upon further investigation, Jack knew this book would be his companion in his fight against the system (or whatever he was going to call it). Maybe Jack's reading war in his mind was finally over. He would show all those who doubted him that he could pay attention to something for more than five minutes and that he could focus on learning for once in his life and that he could—

[20] compelled: to feel forced to move forward

Oh, a fly!

Wait, what?

The bell was ringing. Jack quickly checked out his book and began to head toward his next class. He was walking tall and had the feeling that he could take on the entire world and climb any obstacle, …uh-h-h-h …reality set in when he saw Lenny and was quickly deflated.[21]

* * *

Meanwhile, Madeline Winthrop sat in the living room watching TV. She got home two hours before Nate got home. It wasn't until 30 minutes later that Jack got home. She was watching what appeared to be one of her favorite shows—"Sesame Street." Suddenly, she applied a concerned look on her face and went to her father and asked him, "Wheah ith Thethame Thtweet?"

Her father replied, "I think Sesame Street is in New York, Maddie," in his usual condescending way.

Maddie then proceeded to walk away, content[22] with his answer. Then she muttered, "I know wheah you live, Cookie Monsteaw!" As she began plotting to kidnap Cookie Monster and "persuade" him to give her all his cookies, she decided that the Internet was the best way to find his exact address. When she walked into the computer room and sat down, she

---

[21] deflated: to make someone feel small in size

[22] content: happy

discovered a problem with her plan—she couldn't read or write. To add insult to injury, her arms were too short to reach the buttons to turn on the computer. She decided that Cookie Monster would have to wait… for now.

Just then, Mr. Winthrop walked into the computer room with a strange paper in his hand. He explained to her that due to the fact that she had been so good in kindergarten, her teacher had given her an excellent review. He explained that the paper in his hand was a report card, and that she was doing mighty fine at school.

Maddie began to question what "mighty fine at school" meant in kindergarten. *What could they possibly be judging her on?*, she thought. But Maddie didn't care. Maddie just knew her plan had worked. She had bribed her teacher with a macaroni portrait of herself, and she had succeeded beautifully.

Her father explained that her reward was a trip to the toy store and asked her if she wanted to go since he was able to come home early from work.

Maddie jumped up and down excited and ran to her room to put on her favorite princess dress.

Meanwhile, the employees at the toy store had no idea who and what was coming their way. The store owner had trained his employees that if they ever saw Maddie Winthrop come into the store that they were to go into the back room and get the Barbara Ann doll that she would likely ask to see.

As Maddie and her father walked through the automatic sliding doors, one of the teenage employees warned the others.

"It's Maddie Winthrop! Guys! Maddie Winthrop is back!"

As Maddie closely investigated each and every aisle, making sure the desired contents were in their designated place, she noticed a flaw. She went to one of the checkout counters, and explained the error to the employee.

"I know I didn't just come all the way hewe to find out that thewe's no mow Bawbawa Ann dolls."

The store employee was prepared for her sassy question and said, "Let me check the back for you Miss Maddie."

Maddie's eyes opened wide when the toy store employees emerged with the "Brushie Teeth" Barbara Ann doll.

Even though the Barbara Ann dolls had been removed from the shelves to make room for newer products—they always kept a Barbara Ann doll in the store in case Maddie Winthrop arrived.

"Humpf," replied Maddie. "I supplose that will work" and her father bought the doll.

Exiting the shopping center, Maddie's father drove by the toy store and from her booster seat, Maddie looked back at the toy store and said, "I will wetuwn."

Chapter 5:
Reports

Back at his Middle School, Jack was having a little "chat" with his counselor. Counselor Freuderstein asked, "Jack! Are these reports by Lenny Stevens and his friends true?"

"What kind of reports?" Jack replied.

"They claim that you went up to them and said,

'I'm going to sic[23] Madeline on you!'"

Jack sat back in his chair, smirked, and said, "One must be severely paranoid to go around making empty threats about a 6 year-old girl, Mrs. Freuderstein."

"Well, that's what they said you did. Empty or otherwise, you did make a threat to Lenny."

"In my defense though, you will not believe how well it worked."

"Jack! Whether it worked is not the point. The point is that we don't go around threatening people at our school."

"Sooooo, are you going to punish me?"

"Detention tonight. Be there or else."

Miss Robertson wasn't going to be there to get Jack out of detention this time.

Ms. Stiche has a really big nose.

* * *

Jack's feeling of invincibility[24] had changed to… whatever the opposite of invincibility might be. As he trudged to his next class, he quickly decided that he was too stupid to successfully master the Bradburyian Challenge, and gave up on it. Instead of reading like a maniac during homeroom as he had planned, he resigned to doodle away the time in his notebook. His notebook was covered in doodles, and he incessantly[25] was doodling during every class period. As Jack did most days, he doodled his way through the rest of the school day and then he was off to detention.

* * *

[23] sic: slang to get someone to attack, to go after forcefully

[24] invincibility: courageous, feeling strong

[25] incessantly: unending, continuously

Meanwhile, back at home, there was a revenge plot brewing. Nate Winthrop ran over to Lenny's house, making sure he was unseen, he looked back to find his sister, Madeline. She was rushing over on her tiny little feet, ever so cutely, carrying a big bag of paint-filled water balloons in her tiny little arms. He had brought a ladder and positioned it so the top of it was resting upon Lenny's roof, and then proceeded to climb. Nate looked down at his demon-hearted sister and asked, "Where's Jack? I didn't see him get off the bus."

She replied, "Jack has detention."

"Wow. Ms. Stiche is really going to town on handing out those detentions."

"Not Ms. Stiths. The lady counselow."

"Really? What did he do?"

"Jack made empty thweats at the tawget."

"What did he say?"

"He ted tat he was gonna tic me on him. He must have fowgotten tat my thewvices awe valid on ow awound ouw pwopewty only. And if it wewen't for my showt body and this cuwsid wisp, I would be able to thneak into the school and be able to help him at any time. Like a ninja."

"Yeah, yeah. Again with the ninja! Just give me the water balloons! What color is the paint again?"

"You just want to heaw me thay it."

"Say it anyway!"

Sigh.

"Lellow."

"Hahahaha! It's just so cute!"

"You do wealize I could thnap you like a twig."

"You know every so often you say that thing about a twig, and I must say, it does make me feel very uncomfortable. "

"Thowwy. Thowwy. Help me up Bwew Wabbit."

Jack called Nate Brer Rabbit because he was a trickster. After helping the evil little witch up, Nate sat the tiny terror down beside him.

"Hey, Nate?" she asked. "Why awe we doing this again?"

"We're playing a prank on Lenny, because he made a joke about Jack."

"Awen't a pwank and a joke the thame thing?"

"No, no, no, no, no, no. A joke has an audience."

Lenny walked out of his front door to go get the mail.

"A prank, *Sploosh-splat!* has a victim."

Lenny looked at the ladder that went up to his roof. He then looked at Nate grinning down at him. Lenny was about to tell his mom that the neighbor kids splashed a water balloon filled with yellow paint on his head, but when he saw Madeline, he decided to tell her it was aliens. If he told his mother that Madeline had thrown a yellow, paint-filled water balloon on his head, the outcome would most likely be worse than if he were abducted by aliens.

Chapter 6:
Delinquents

In detention, one is expected to do the homework assigned by his or her teachers. But Jack had no such plans. Jack knew what he would do, but first he and all of the other "delinquents"[26] had to listen to Mr. Calloway's lecture on discipline. Jack

---

[26] delinquents: not following and neglecting the rules

internally humored Mr. Calloway by calling his "half-minute tell-off" a "lecture." Mr. Calloway was also the only person who ever called Jack a delinquent, and the only person Jack ever heard use the word "delinquent." Not even Ms. Stiche used that word. Not even "The Therapist" used that word. Jack didn't have any animosity[27] toward "The Therapist." He knew "The Therapist" had a job to do, and that job was to help Jack. The only problem Jack saw was that he rarely agreed with "The Therapist's" suggestions, such as when he told Jack to view his difficulties as "challenges," and to make a goal of overcoming these "challenges." He recommended that Jack should even keep a record or scorecard of his efforts. It was usually around this time that Jack began to tune out "The Therapist."

Although Mr. Calloway was in charge of torturing Jack in detention, Jack did feel sorry for him at times. For one thing, Jack pitied Mr. Calloway for having the emotional part of his brain replaced with a lemon, and for the fact that his canine teeth hooked down like fangs. Jack thought that he might as well feel compassion for the half-robot, half-saber-toothed tiger, somewhat human teacher, Mr. Calloway.

In a monotone voice, Mr. Calloway began to give his "lecture."

"You are all in here for good reasons, and you should all learn a big lesson from this experience. It makes me happy to know that all of you are able to learn your lessons from your bad deeds."

Apparently, this made Mr. Calloway so happy that he decided to engage in "Smile-Phase I."

---

[27] animosity: anger, a strong dislike

Something inside Jack's head was yelling at him about Mr. Calloway's teeth.

His head screamed, *Ask him about being a vampire! Ask him! Ask him!* Then it said, *Tell him that you're very happy that you could have an oral conversation.*

Jack almost did, but then he realized that Mr. Calloway had already raised both of his arms in a plank formation and, without bending his knees or twisting his ankles, stomped out of the classroom to get his bolts tightened, hence "Robot-Phase 2."

Jack began to wonder...*hmm he wondered what his family was doing at that moment. His mom was probably looking for ingredients for his lunch—most likely going to cattle ranches and asking the farmers if their cows had an awful lot of fiber today. His dad was probably doing what he does best: lying in bed and watching Madeline. Although it was more likely that Madeline was watching him. Nate was probably working out some sort of master plan to get back at Lenny, which most likely involved water balloons filled with yellow paint. Madeline was probably sharpening her Barbara Ann doll's toothbrush.*

Oh, no, it's already happening again... I just need to rest and get all of these random, swirling thoughts out of my head.

So Jack put his head in his folded arms and drifted into dreamland. Only this time, his dreams weren't filled with the victorious vanquishing[28] of villains. This time, Jack was in some sort of world made of notebook paper. He realized that all of this notebook paper was his notebook paper filled with his doodles—the one with him knocking Lenny's head off with a club, tying dynamite to Ms. Stiche's nose, and riding on a unicorn to the crystal palace. He recognized all of these drawings as his own. In his most recent drawings, he was a hero. But in his older drawings, there was some sort of darkness about him—some sort of evil radiance,[29] like the kind that you get every time you see the black garbage bin. *What could be causing these changes*, he thought. *My Book-O's? The meds? Do they actually work?*

As Jack continued to investigate some of these drawings, he felt as if the cartoons of himself were staring back at him, which was weird because the eyes were just big, black dots and they had no pupils. Maybe it was just one of those feelings. But then he noticed that the drawings of him were starting to swell and move and walk toward him. And they stared at him with those big, black eyes—like a doll's eyes—never ceasing to stare into the soul of their prey. Suddenly, Jack found himself carrying the laser sword of Oga, and he could use it to defend himself from the evil Jack clones. With one heroic swipe, the laser sword sliced straight through one of the clones, and it did absolutely nothing. After all, it was just a light. But what did happen was that the Jack clones zeroed in on him the way zombies do. They came closer, closer, closer until suddenly… detention was over.

[28] vanquishing: to conquer, to defeat

[29] radiance: brightness, full of light

"I'm very upset with you, young man," Mr. Calloway said to Jack as he woke up. "Sleeping in detention when you should be doing homework! I should give you another detention, but you are not the only person who fell asleep."

Jack said to Mr. Calloway, "You think you're mad?! Wait until my mother gets a hold of me!" Jack could already picture his mother's eyes, which glared like a doll's eyes, never ceasing[30] to stare into the soul of their prey.

On his way out of detention, Jack began to ask himself whether dolls actually stared into the soul of their prey... His train of thought was interrupted, however, when a car pulled up and he found himself staring into the eyes of the beast.

[30] ceasing: stopping, ending

Chapter 7:
Such As...

"Get in here now, young man!" The mom clock was very angry.

Wow, Mom is angry with a capital G. Ha ha ha, grammar joke. Good one, Brain! Jack thought.

He was so busy congratulating himself that he almost forgot he was staring into the eyes of the beast, who proceeded to take him by the neck—or maybe it was the hair—into the car. She went into "Angry Mom" mode and he suffered all the way home. Surprisingly, Jack felt more damaged from his mom's oral abuse than from the injustices done to his neck or hair.

Once they arrived at home, she continued saying

things such as, "I'm very upset with you, Jack!" and "What were you thinking?"

Jack played the guilty teenager card and answered every question with, "I don't know. I'm sorry. Yeah." Jack looked at the clock to give him some sort of excuse to not look into the eyes of the beast. The clock said 4:51 p.m. Jack's bedtime was 8:30 p.m. He only had 3½ more painful hours plus 9 minutes of this never-ending nagging. Jack knew that getting sent to detention meant no video games or TV or even watching grass grow.

* * *

"I really did watch grass grow once, and it was awesome!" Jack exclaimed for no apparent purpose.

"Watching grass grow was awesome?" inquired Nate. "Sorry I asked, I was just trying to see the different ways one could entertain himself if he were to be grounded... like you."

"Shaddap rabbait! What if the gwass thange colows ath it gwew? And it gwew and when ith wath done gwowing it yooked yike a wainbow?" philosophized[31] Madeline.

Yes! Jack thought. He marveled at the idea of heterochromal vegetation. Grass that changed color as it grew, and in the end it made a big rainbow. He imagined it in his mind. *I shall create such grass*, he thought. Grass that will dazzle the entire world, and I will be known as the grass man! THE MAN WHO RENOVATED GRASS! This is stupid. He may have dismissed the challenge of creating kaleidoscopic[32]

[31] philosophized: to think, to speculate
[32] kaleidoscopic: changing and shifting colors into form or patterns

grass, but it did remind him of a different challenge that he gave himself: the Bradburyian Challenge.

At first, Jack was excited to start this new challenge, but then he started to think. He started to think about the detention and what he did in the detention. And he remembered he couldn't even do homework in detention. He questioned his ability to complete the Bradburyian Challenge. He finally decided that it was too much for him, and that he was unable to finish the *The Machineries of Joy*. So, even before beginning, he resigned himself to give up, and he didn't learn anything at all.

THE END.

* * *

What? Wait...the editor just informed me that the story needs to be longer, so you can just ignore the ending above. Here's the real resolution...

Chapter 8:
As Fast as Her Feet Could Carry Her

Ms. Stiche was in her office packing up and getting ready to go home for the weekend. That's when she noticed a document that she did not recognize on her desk. When she lifted the paper, she realized that there were, in fact, several documents that she did not recognize on her desk. All of the documents were professionally written by doctors, psychiatrists, and therapists, and every one of them referenced the topic of Attention Deficit Hyperactivity Disorder. Many of them were prescriptions, theses, and articles. Each one of them treated ADHD as a very sensitive and very real diagnosis.

"Now, who could have left these here?" Ms. Stiche asked herself. She looked outside, and she saw Miss Robertson running as fast as her feet could carry her. Ms. Stiche knew that Anne Robertson always had a sorely misguided soft spot for Jack Winthrop, but Ms. Stiche knew better and thinking to herself, *There is no real ADHD! That's just an excuse some parents give to their children, when in reality, they're just bad students, right?*

Ms. Stiche's questioning of her own opinions was delayed when Principal Feldkircher walked in her door. He was about to leave as well. He told Ms. Stiche, "Verna, I'm heading out for the night, so I will see you Monday." He noticed the stack of papers on her desk and said, "That's a fair amount of papers to grade. You must be planning on a long night." He walked up to Ms. Stiche's desk and noticed that they were all about ADHD. Mr. Feldkircher groaned. "Are you on one of your ADHD rants again?" he asked her.

Ms. Stiche replied, "No. Anne left these here. She's still trying to convince me that ADHD is an actual diagnosis."

"Well, I am staying out of that one. I think I will be on my way!" said Mr. Feldkircher.

As he walked out of the classroom, Ms. Stiche looked at the papers one more time. She grabbed the stack of ADHD articles to take home to read over the weekend, but then decided against it and set the stack back down on her desk. She repeated this process a few times, until she finally decided to take just a few articles with her.

* * *

The next day had proven to be a particularly difficult day for Jack. He looked down at his English homework. He was angry at himself. Very angry. So angry that he decided to punish himself. His punishment was to complete the entire essay. Jack carried out his punishment beautifully and completed the essay in 30 minutes. He looked at the essay and reread it. Then he had Nate read it and then his mom. Jack knew he had punished himself well, when they all told him that it was a rather fine essay.

Jack told himself, "*Ha! Now you've written an excellent and well-educated essay in 30 minutes! What do you say to that?*"

Jack was still upset that he had completed a very good essay in 30 minutes. Then he realized that he had completed a very good essay in 30 minutes. He looked at the essay, which he titled "The Elements of Civil Rights." He looked at it again and again and again. Each time he read it, he thought it got better and better.

Jack was inspired. He thought, *If I can do this, I can finish a collection of science fiction short stories in three weeks.* He marveled at himself and as he marveled, he was unaware of his mom creeping up behind him. Dolls really do creep up behind their prey instead of looking into their soul.

She told Jack, "Since you've done such a good job at homework, you can go play video games."

Jack thought, *YES!*

But then he realized that he didn't want to play video games. He wanted to read The Machineries of Joy. So he went upstairs to his room, picked up the book, sat in bed, and... stared at the book. He then proceeded to slowly start to... read. Jack felt as if it was the first time in his life he had ever done that, and it probably was. Reading the book made Jack feel empowered. He felt like he was king of the world, as if everyone should be looking up to him.

Chapter 9:
I'd Rather Be Awake

"It's time to go to bed," Jack's mom said from the doorway. So he put his book on the floor as his mom turned out the lights and said good night. Jack made sure that his alarm clock was set and tried to go to sleep, but he couldn't. He felt that he would rather be awake. This was not unusual for Jack, and the following day's fatigue[33] was often the reason that he didn't do very well in P.E.

But this time, his alertness was for a different reason. It was because of the book, *The Machineries of Joy*. It beckoned[34] him. At first, when something beckons, you might hesitate, but Jack knew that the beckoning was for a good reason. He should obey it.

Then he thought, *The Beckoning. That would be a great title for a movie or a book!* He was about to go into a whole attention deficit episode, but then he reminded himself, *No, Jack! You must not give in to the impulse.* And he agreed. *Yes, Jack, yes—we need to read the book—yes, the book. We must complete the challenge that we set for ourselves. It's time to be a man—and read that book. Yeah, let's do it!*

"Jack, quiet down," called Nate from the other room. Jack realized then that he was talking to himself. He was having another "episode"—something that he was just warning himself not to do. This made him feel discouraged and made him doubt his ability to complete the Bradburyian Challenge.

But I am a new Jack, he thought. And the new Jack needed to summon the courage to face his challenges head on.

Perhaps "The Therapist" was right, he thought aloud. *Perhaps there was hope he could set and achieve a goal. Perhaps the whole day was an illusion[35] and there really was no Therapist at all…*

---

[33] fatigue: tiredness, weary
[34] beckoned: called, signaled, lured

FOCUS!!! he thought.

So, he looked at the book again, picked it up, and started reading it. He read for a whole 30 minutes. Even though it seemed like he had been reading for 24 hours straight, it struck him that all the words made sense and the images he saw were from someone else's fantasy—not his own. This gave him a strange feeling, one he had not felt often enough.

Was this "accomplishment?" he thought.

He could sense a smile emerging[36] and couldn't resist touching his face as he closed the book, adjusted his pillow, and prepared to sleep, knowing that he would complete the Bradburyian challenge. He knew that he could, and he knew that he would.

His mom opened the door to check on him and watched him for a second. She hadn't seen him so peaceful and relaxed since a time when… she could not remember.

"Good night, Jack," she said. " I love you."

"Good night, Mom. I love you, too," said Jack as she closed the door.

"Beep! Beep!" he said with a giggle.

The door opened quickly, "What, son?"

"Nothing. G'night," he said.

Beep.

---

[35] illusion: produces a false sense of reality

[36] emerging: developing

4114U
(Information For You!)

Written by:

Lewis S. Ribner, Ph.D. - Clincal Psychologist

Carey Averill, M.Ed. - Educator

Susan Van Zanten, M.A.Ed.- Educator

Kids: Our intent is that you will read through this 4114U section with your parent or guardian. Please read and discuss the tips and tools provided as you process this information together. Our goals are for you to create a game plan that will help you navigate through your struggles with ADHD.

Parents: A parent's job is to give their children the tools needed to navigate, and to be active participants in solving problems that will invariably come their way in life. Whether your child is having test anxiety or having trouble focusing at school, let them know that you are there for them and they aren't alone.

Hopefully, this book will open up a wonderful world of communication where together, you and your child can safely navigate and sail through this tough situation together.

Action Steps to Help Families Emotionally

Written by:
Lewis S. Ribner, Ph.D. - Clinical Psychologist

What is ADD/ADHD?

What was once called Attention Deficit Disorder (ADD) is now called Attention Deficit Hyperactivity Disorder (ADHD). There are three types of ADHD:

1. Attention Deficit Hyperactivity Disorder, Predominantly Inattentive Type,
2. Attention Deficit Hyperactivity Disorder, Predominantly Hyperactive/Impulsive Type
3. Attention Deficit Hyperactivity Disorder, Combined Type (inattention and hyperactivity/ impulsivity).

According to the DSM-IV (a book used by doctors and other professionals to help understand certain problems), the following list describes what people with ADHD might experience:

Inattention

(a) often fails to give close attention to details or makes careless mistakes in schoolwork, work or other activities

(b) often has difficulty sustaining attention in tasks or play activity

(c) often does not seem to listen when spoken to directly

(d) often does not follow through on instructions and fails to finish schoolwork, chores or duties in the workplace (not due to oppositional behavior or failure to understand instructions)

(e) often has difficulty organizing tasks and activities

(f) often avoids, dislikes, or is reluctant to engage in tasks that require sustained mental effort (such as schoolwork or homework)

(g) often looses things necessary for tasks or activities (E.g., toys, school assignments, pencils, books, or tools)

(h) is often easily distracted by extraneous stimuli

(i) is often forgetful in daily activities

Hyperactivity

(a) often fidgets with hands or feet or squirms in seat

(b) often leaves seat in classroom or in other situations in which remaining seated is expected

(c) often runs about or climbs excessively in situations in which it is inappropriate (in adolescents or adults, may be limited to subjective feelings of restlessness)

(d) often has difficulty playing or engaging in leisure activities quietly

(e) is often "on the go" or often acts as if "driven by a motor"

(f) often talks excessively

Impulsivity

(a) often blurts out answers before questions have
    been completed

(b) often has difficulty awaiting turn

(c) often interrupts or intrudes on others (e.g., butts
    into conversations or games)

What Causes ADHD?

We really don't know the exact cause of ADHD,
but professionals believe it is most likely caused by
any or all of the following:

Brain chemistry:

The chemicals in the brain that control our ability
to pay attention and control our behavior are not
balanced.

Genes:

ADHD runs in families and some children are
more likely to get ADHD if someone else in their
family has it.

Environment:

Certain things that may happen when a mom is
pregnant or a child is very young may contribute to
developing ADHD.

More Information for Parents

Often, ADHD first becomes apparent when someone is required to concentrate more than before. This may happen as early as kindergarten when children are first asked to follow social rules, in early grades when they are asked to concentrate on desk work or homework, or perhaps later in life when demands of school or work increase.

Many parents experience the frustration and emotional upheaval caused by living with a child with ADHD. In general, parenting children is a difficult task that can bring us from one end of the emotional spectrum to the other. Raising children brings out the extreme of emotions from lack of control, frustration, anger, sadness, or pain, to joy, happiness, warmth, pride, and love. Living with an ADHD child exaggerates those emotions many times over.

Parents of ADHD children will say things like, "but my child is so smart," or "my child knows better," when wondering why their child has or hasn't done something. It is important to understand that ADHD interferes with self-regulation and is a disorder of performance, not a lack of skill or intelligence. These children have problems with self-control. They may have poor problem-solving behavior, limited emotional self-control, and poor social behavior.

Children with this disorder may also show signs of oppositional/defiant behavior, which may at some point, lead to conduct disorder. These children have difficulty following rules and taking responsibility for their behavior. They frequently blame others for their mistakes or misbehavior, they constantly test and push limits, and they are often angry and argumentative.

These children often appear to invest more energy in the argument than in its outcome, and they are excellent at getting others, especially their parents, hooked into the process of arguing.

How to Diagnose and Treat ADHD

Diagnosis and treatment of ADHD is a comprehensive process involving cooperation of parents, teachers, and experienced health professionals. Medical and family history, information provided by parents and teachers through the use of certain questionnaires and personal interviews, will help provide the information necessary to make the diagnosis. Administration of a brief continuous performance test (CPT) is helpful to confirm or rule out the diagnosis and to determine other possible causes of reported symptoms.

Once an appropriate diagnosis has been made, the treatment of ADHD involves education, medication, and development of appropriate strategies to learn to function more effectively. Children with ADHD are often delayed developmentally in their communication skills, social functioning, and other areas of performance. Therefore, establishing a model in which they are seen as in need of special assistance is important. Making changes in the child's environment to assist him/her to best deal with his/her disability is essential. Parent training, teacher training and child training, are necessary to manage this disorder and to help these children feel better about themselves and feel more successful overall. Though there are some alternatives to medication (neurofeedback, Interactive Metronome [interactivemetronome.com], diet etc.) most treatment for ADHD involves an appropriate evaluation for medicine. Stimulant medications such as Concerta®, Ritalin®, Adderall®, and Vyvanse® are the primary medicines prescribed. Stratera is a, non-stimulant medication that seems effective for some individuals. There are various preparations, with varying side effects, and while they are usually quite safe to use, their effectiveness depends on the individual, the situation where they are being used (school, work, etc.) and on the skill of the person prescribing the medicine. Other medications such as antidepressants and those used to treat hypertension are also prescribed at times. While using medication sounds frightening to some parents and children, medicines can make the difference between good and happier function and continuing frustration. The point is that you must work with an experienced professional when using medicines. The beneficial effects of medication for ADHD have been known for many years. They include but are not limited to increased attention span and concentration, decreased impulsivity, decreased motor activity, decreased aggressiveness, increased compliance, improved fine motor skills, improved peer relations and improved participation in sports. The prescribing physician should inform patients of possible side effects and should assist in providing education regarding myths and realities concerning these medicines.

Who Can Help?

Your doctor or your child's school may guide you to experienced health professionals dealing with the diagnosis and treatment of attention problems. There are some excellent books on ADHD available at libraries and bookstores. A favorite is *Driven to Distraction*, by Dr. Hallowell. There are also free community support groups for persons and families with ADHD. CHADD is one of these. There are chapters of this organization in most major cities and they have a website as well (chadd.org). It is often very helpful to meet other families facing the same kinds of challenges to get ideas as well as support.

Teachers and schools can also help. Federal law requires that public schools make appropriate accommodations for students with ADHD which may include preferential seating, giving untimed tests, keeping school work at school (not sending it home), and keeping an eye out for learning problems (dyslexia, math difficulties, etc). A colleague, Dr. David Weiss, has listed the following "Ten Commandments for Teachers of ADD Children", which applies to families and employers too:

1. Understand that ADD is a handicapping condition, and the nature of the ADD child's deficits.

2. Be tough as nails about rules, but always stay calm and positive.

3. Speak clearly, in brief understandable sentences.

4. Provide immediate and consistent feedback (consequences) regarding behavior, as well as academic success. Use as much positive reinforcement as possible.

5. Run a predictable and organized classroom.

6. Don't overwhelm the ADD child with a large volume of work. Go for quality, not quantity. Keep assignments to the minimum length sufficient to demonstrate mastery.

7. Look for the ADD child's strengths and build on them.

8. Help the ADD child organize his desk area and materials.

9. Closely monitor the child's behavior without being intrusive.

10. Maintain a good sense of humor!

Parents & Kids: What Can You Do? Some Tips for Parents and Children

(1) **Exercise, diet, and sleep** are important factors affecting ADHD. Daily aerobic exercise, a low carbohydrate/ higher protein diet, and a consistent sleep pattern (8-10 hours/night are strongly recommended.

(2) **Communication:**
(a) Parents need to make sure they are face to face with their child when giving instructions. Yelling upstairs to a child who is involved in doing something is more than likely a guarantee for your request not to be heard.

(b) Parents need to communicate clearly with each other to enable greater structure and consistency at home. Clear, reasonable expectations and consequences are helpful.

(c) **Communicate clearly** with teachers and school personnel about your child's difficulties and needs. Within certain limits, schools are required to provide accommodations to better provide for your child's academic and behavioral needs. The only way the school will know what your child needs is by you providing appropriate information to the right people.

(3) **Reminders**…we cannot trust that our ADHD children will remember anything. Parents and children need to write things down…we can safely operate on the assumption that if things are not written, they will most likely not be remembered. Let's help our children by providing reasonable reminders. It is important to help them set up planners, schedules, etc. and please try hard to have reasonable, realistic expectations of your particular child's abilities.

(4) **Ask for help!** Psychologists/Therapists, Educational Therapists/Coaches and teachers are excellent resources to assist with learning problems, emotional and behavioral issues and building skills to learn to compensate for deficits. Parents and children need to depend on friends for help. Students should always make an effort to have at least one person in every class that can help provide missing information (notes, assignments to be done, due dates for assignments, etc.) and parents will make themselves feel better if they make an effort to seek support from their friends.

Certain information presented above was extracted from a previous article written by Lewis S. Ribner, Ph.D. and Joshua Feder, M.D.

Action Steps to Help Families Socially

Written by: Carey Averill, M.Ed. - Educator

ADHD and the School Environment?

Working with children with ADHD in a classroom setting can be challenging, so teachers need to be familiar with strategies and useful tips in order to minimize the frustration for all parties. Most importantly, students struggling with ADHD need to know teachers are there to help. Creating a classroom environment to help channel the energy of all students is essential. Maximizing student involvement is a critical component to all teaching, but extremely beneficial to students who struggle with inattentiveness.

Suggestions for Teacher Instruction include the following:

• Provide a daily outline/itinerary of what will be covered each class period/day. Refer to the chart throughout the day so they can easily follow the routine of the classroom.

• Enable students to actively participate throughout each lesson using white boards, response cards, partner discussions, movement, song, etc. Break all lessons up into smaller chucks so students can frequently respond. Sitting too long is an invitation for disruption.

- Use whole brain learning techniques to engage students, instructing in small segments throughout each lesson. This allows practice, discussion, and routine feedback.

- When giving instructions or stating important facts, have the whole class repeat the information (as opposed to one student.)

- Provide "brain breaks" when students seem restless.

- Make sure every teacher has a copy of the child's 504 which provides specified accommodations. Ensure meetings, monitoring, and programs are being followed as directed.

- Encourage open lines of communication between teachers, parents, and administrators.

Suggestions for Socialization:

Students with ADHD may experience many difficulties with peer relationships. Based on the needs of each individual, social skills training in a small group setting may need to be implemented throughout the school year to help learn appropriate skills. Set objectives need to be shared with the teacher so that reinforcement can occur. Other classroom objectives that may be useful include the following:

- In working on social skills, multimedia offers programs that teach social skills in authentic situations.

• Parental training is useful to learn new techniques that differ depending upon the age of the student.

• Implementing rewards and consequences for appropriate peer interactions is quite effective. Simply placing a child with ADHD in a setting with other children does not improve their social skills interaction.

• Prior to small group interaction, teachers need to verbalize what appropriate discussions/interactions look like and sound like and what is inappropriate. Modeling desired behavior is a key technique for children who are still learning social skills.

• Pairing students up with other helpful students who have keen social skills and can kindly correct inappropriate behavior is beneficial for all parties. Meet with the pairing to set expectations and obtain parental permission. Limit the time commitment so that both parties can achieve success. Also working with an older peer is an effective tool to help with social skills.

• Teach social skills through role-playing and observation. Select only one or two skills that you want to improve upon, ask students to take on roles, provide feedback, and practice the new desired skills. This can become a safe avenue for ADHD students. Such practice can then be played out time and again until you feel they have mastered a skill. A fun addition to this activity includes videotaping the modeling behavior. Having the students view and critique the videos as the school year progresses enables the student to view the actions and watch the behavioral cues time and again. Your class will soon have its own video library on social skills that benefit every student in the class/school.

• Cooperative groups also work well for students with ADHD.

• Accompany your student outside for recess to watch how others play and interact. Have a discussion on appropriate behavior. Encourage them to try such behaviors.

Suggestions for Classroom Management:

• Assign students with ADHD to sit near the front of the room, closest to instruction. The less distractors, the easier it is to remain focused.

• Do not place students with ADHD near windows or doors where there is constant activity.

• Build in time after each lesson for the students to write down their assignments in their binders/homework planner, etc. This should not be rushed as the bell is ringing for dismissal.

• Assign a responsible, organized student to help others with these needed skills.

• Encourage movement in your room. If they need to stand or walk, allow them the freedom as long as it doesn't disturb the class.

Suggestions for Students with ADHD:

Kids:

- Have an on-going discussion about the importance of learning. Have students with ADHD create a list of the strategies that seem to work well so they have ownership. This sets the stage for all parties.

- Agree on how you will privately signal them to get back on task (rather than calling out their inappropriate attention to everyone.) Ideas include a tap on their desk, placing a sticky note on their desk, or a tap on their hand.

- Eye contact is essential.

- Students with ADHD need to know and hear they are successful, so be sure to provide positive feedback in regards to their behavior.

- While sitting, try a fidget frog or stress ball.

- Let students know who to turn to if they are feeling frustrated or experiencing emotional or behavioral issues. Visit the school's guidance counselor to set the stage of a safe place to talk. This is also a good resource for books and information on dealing with this disorder. Guidance counselors may also offer small group sessions involving anger management, organizational skills, study skills, etc.

- Help the student create a team of people that can offer help and support such as fellow classmates, teachers, guidance counselor, school nurse, coaches, mentors, parents, and siblings.

Learning Styles

Everyone processes information and learns in a slightly different manner. As such, people tend to favor differing learning styles and techniques. Some people have a dominant style they prefer while others have a mix. As we grow, our preferences in how we learn may change or we may strengthen the way in which we learn best. Research shows that each learning style uses different parts of the brain and the more parts we use, the better we remember information.

When identifying a student's primary learning style, you should discover how each individual:
- takes in information
- processes information
- relates information

Children may experience great amounts of frustration because they were taught methods that were in direct opposition to their strengths. Finding success relies heavily on identifying how one learns and then taking those skills and applying them to the educational setting.

There are seven main learning styles that educators try to incorporate into their lessons in order to reach the many different learning styles of their students. These seven styles include:

•Visual (spatial)
- preferences for pictures, images, and spatial understanding

•Aural (auditory)
- preference for sound and music

•Verbal (linguistic)
- preference for using words in speech and writing

•Physical (kinesthetic)
- preference for using your body or sense of touch

•Logical (mathematical)
-preference for using logic or reasoning

•Social (interpersonal)
-preference for learning in groups or with others

•Solitary (intrapersonal)
-preference to work alone and use self-study

Once you have determined your preferred style, you can incorporate techniques that are best suited to match your needs. In knowing your strengths, you can enhance your learning and improve your overall performance.

Action Steps to Help Families Spiritually and Holistically

Foreword written by: Colleen C. Ster, KidsGames Manager

When a person goes through a difficult time in life, they may often question their belief system or their house worship. They may wonder why they have to suffer and feel paralyzed from ADHD. According to Dr. Harold Koenig's book, *The Healing Power of Faith*, his research indicates that when people are faced with health problems or life challenges, it is the individuals with strong belief systems that have the best overall, positive recovery. When people can believe in something bigger than themselves, they can often heal faster and experience less pain.

As you experience the frustration of ADHD, you need to know that there is hope. Nobody—adult or child—is strong enough to navigate through ADHD alone. Having a strong connection with others and a belief system can help you work through this difficult time and heal.

From the *God's Calling* book by A.J. Russell, it eloquently combines the emotional, social, and spiritual aspect of healing. In the book's passage "Secret of Healing" it says:

> "Love the busy life. It is a joy-filled life. I love you both and bid you be of good cheer. Take your fill of joy in the Spring.
>
> Live outside whenever possible. Sun and air are My great healing forces, and that inward Joy that changes...to a pure healthy life-giving flow.
>
> Never forget that real healing of body, mind, and Spirit come from within, from the close loving contact of your spirit with My Spirit."

Written by:
Susan Van Zanten, M.A.Ed. - Educator

7 Types of Intelligences

Professor Howard Gardner of Harvard University says that unlike traditional theories of intelligence that focus on one, single general intelligence, people instead have different ways of thinking and learning. According to this theory, he states, "we are all able to know the world through language, logical-mathematical analysis, spatial representation, musical thinking, the use of the body to solve problems or to make things, an understanding of other individuals, and an understanding of ourselves." While this may be a challenge for the education system to address, a more broad approach of allowing students to learn might be a more effective way to assess a student's abilities. These are the 7 types of intelligences and suggestions to how they might learn best:

• Visual-Spatial
- These students think in terms of physical space, as do architects and sailors. They are very aware of their environments. They like to draw, do jigsaw puzzles, read maps, and daydream. They can be taught through drawings, verbal, and physical imagery. Tools include models, graphics, charts, videoconferencing, drawings, 3-D modeling, multimedia, videos, photographs, television, and texts with pictures/charts/graphs.

• Bodily - kinesthetic

- These students use the body effectively, like a dancer or a surgeon. They have a keen sense of body awareness. They like movement, making things, and touching. They communicate well through body language and can be taught through physical activity, hands-on learning, acting out, and role playing. Tools include equipment and real objects.

• Musical

- These students show sensitivity to rhythm and sound. They love music, but they are also sensitive to sounds in their environments. They may study better with music in the background. They can be taught by turning lessons into lyrics, speaking rhythmically, tapping out time. Tools include musical instruments, music, radio, stereo, CD-ROM, and multimedia.

• Interpersonal

- These students understand and interact well with others. They learn through interaction. They have many friends, empathy for others, and street smarts. They can be taught through group activities, seminars, and dialogues. Tools include the telephone, audio conferencing, time and attention from the instructor, video conferencing, writing, computer conferencing, and e-mail.

• Intrapersonal

- These students understand their own interests and goals. They tend to shy away from others. They are in tune with their inner feelings, have wisdom, intuition and motivation, as well as, a strong will, confidence and opinions. They can be taught through independent study, and introspection. Tools include books, creative materials, diaries, privacy, and time. They are the most independent of the learners.

• Linguistic

- These students use words effectively. They have highly developed auditory skills and often think in words. They like reading, playing word games, making up poetry or stories. They can be taught by encouraging them to say and see words, and read books together. Tools include computers, games, multimedia, books, tape recorders, and lecture.

• Logical

- Mathematical: Students are reasoning and calculating. They think conceptually, abstractly, and are able to see and explore patterns and relationships. They like to experiment, solve puzzles, ask cosmic questions. They can be taught through logic games, investigations, and mysteries. They need to learn and form concepts before they can deal with details.

How Nutrition Affects the Way We Think?

Studies have shown that in addition to helping protect us from heart disease and cancer, a healthy diet can also protect the brain and ward off potential mental disorders. It has been proven that deficiencies in Omega-3 fatty acids (found in salmon, walnuts, and kiwi fruit) have been associated with increased risk of several mental disorders such as ADHD, bipolar disorder, and schizophrenia. When given increased amounts of Omega-3, studies confirmed that children performed better in reading and writing and displayed fewer behavioral problems in the classroom.

Nutrition is an elemental aspect in developing the mind to its full potential. When the body is unhealthy, the mind cannot function properly. God created the human body to function in a distinct way and when the body experiences physical, spiritual, or environmental disturbances, the body becomes compromised. Paying attention to what goes in your body can have drastic affects on what goes out.

Superfoods to Help you Focus

We all know we feel better with a good meal in our bodies, but when it comes to knowing what foods give us the most focus power each day, things get a bit hazy. Here are foods to help improve your focus.

Spirulina is a green filled with B12, protein and iron make it one of the best focus foods you can eat. You can add it to a morning smoothie.

Cacao is a tasty supplement that has a high source of magnesium which helps lower stress and anxiety. Cacao is a wonderful chocolate addition to a morning or afternoon smoothie.

Almonds are rich in magnesium, which improves mental focus, reduces stress, and aids in healthy nervous system function.

Fish such as Salmon, Sardines, Tuna, Cod and Mackerel are loaded with protein, minerals and healthy fats.

Leafy greens like kale, spinach, romaine, collards and Swiss chard are some of the best foods for mental focus. Greens are packed with magnesium, iron, B vitamins, protein, fiber, and chlorophyll. Add them to a smoothie or saute them at dinner.

Fats, fats and more fats! But good fats! Olive oil, sunflower oil, coconut oil, and butter are some of the best! Good fats and oils help protect the walls of the brain that are in charge of your mood.

"Brain Food" Recipes

"The Stimulator" Smoothie (non-vegan)

1 cup of frozen blueberries
1 frozen banana
½ cup of kale
½ cup of plain whole yogurt
1 T almond butter
1 scoop of protein powder
1 tsp of cacao
3 dates (for sweetening)
milk

"The Stimulator" Smoothie (vegan)

1 cup of frozen blueberries
1 frozen banana
½ cup of kale
1 T almond butter
1 scoop of plant based protein powder
1 tsp cacao
3 dates
almond milk

Inside the ADHD Brain:
Topic: Can't Slow Down
Written by: Susan Van Zanten M.A.Ed, Illustrated by: Julia Paul-Fishe

Inside the ADHD Brain:
Topic: Not Organized

Inside the ADHD Brain:
Topic: Medicine-Phobia

Inside the ADHD Brain:
Topic: My Mind Is Like Flipping TV Channels

Inside the ADHD Brain:
Topic: "Going Green" - Get Outside
Written by: Colleen C. Ster, Illustrated by: Julia Paul-Fisher

"Green Time"

According to Karen Barrow in ADDitudemag.com, researchers are finding that, "time spent in natural settings, so-called 'green time,' measurably reduces inattentiveness in children with ADHD." "Studies suggest that time spent in nature can help children with ADHD recharge their attention and focus."

Try some of Andrea Faber Taylor's outdoor activities that rejuvenate kids after a long day of sitting still at school:

- Ride a bike
- Join a sports team
- Roam in a wooded area
- Go Fishing
- Camp outside in your backyard
- Jump on a Trampoline
- Take a hike
- Visit a park
- Bird watch
- Build a snow fort
- Throw rocks in lake

(http://www.additudemag.com/adhd/article/8273.html)

About Our Experts:

• Carey Averill, M.Ed.

Middle School Math Teacher and STEM Coordinator for the Richmond Diocese of Catholic Schools at St. John the Apostle in Virginia Beach

Carey Averill is a doctoral candidate at the George Washington University studying Educational Leadership and Policy Studies. She holds a Bachelors in Education from Purdue University and a Masters in School Counseling from Campbell University. With numerous certifications, her passion for math and love of middle school has lead her to teach 6th grade mathematics, pre-algebra and high school Algebra for the Richmond Diocese of Catholic Schools at St. John the Apostle in Virginia Beach. Previous experience includes teaching for the Department of Defense Dependent Schools in numerous states as well as abroad to include Korea, Germany, and Fort Bragg, NC. With such diverse opportunities, Carey has worked with varying age groups all over the globe.

She has two boys who keep her an active participant in basketball, lacrosse, track, and cross country. Her goal is to empower both students and teachers in order to find success both academically as well as in individual endeavors.

• Lewis Ribner, Ph.D.

http://www.docribner.com

Dr. Ribner is a clinical psychologist with over 35 years of experience assisting children, adolescents and adults with behavioral, emotional and relationship difficulties. He dedicated the first 16 years of his career to treating individuals impacted by child sexual abuse. Since then, Dr. Ribner has focused on his passion and special interest in learning and child development, with the goal of helping others learn the skills needed to work at the levels at which they are truly capable. A portion of Dr. Ribner's practice is dedicated to evaluating and treating attention disorders in children, teens and adults. On a more personal level, Dr. Ribner has been married for 37 years to a woman who, as a Social Worker and Attorney, has dedicated much of her professional life to protecting children. He and his wife have two children, a daughter age 32, a Pediatric Physical Therapist working at All Children's Hospital in St. Petersburg, Florida, and a son, age 24, currently working on his Ph.D. in Developmental Psychology at N.Y.U. in New York.

• Susan Van Zanten, M.A.Ed.

Education Specialist at Winston School

Susan has been in the field of education since 1983. As a second grade teacher for the Pasadena City Schools she was responsible for implementing new strategies to the GATE program. After raising her children and completing graduate school, Susan returned to the classroom with a deeper sense of individualized education and a better understanding of how best to meet the needs of the diverse student. Susan obtained a BA in Liberal Arts at Point Loma Nazarene University and an MA in Education, Digital Teaching and Learning from Azusa Pacific University CA teaching credential, Multiple Subject CA teaching credential, Special Education.

Web Links:

- ADD Center for Success
  http://sandiegoadhdcenter.com

- ADDitude Magazine
  http://www.additudemag.com

- American Academy of Child and Adolescent Psychiatry
  (AACAP)
  http://www.aacap.org

- American Academy of Pediatrics (AAP)
  http://aap.org

- Attention Deficit Disorder Association (ADDA)
  http://add.org

- Breath Body Mind - Richard P. Brown, MD and
  Patricia L. Gerbarg, MD
  http://www.breath-body-mind.com/non-drug-treatments-
  for-adhd.php

- Children and Adults with Attention-Deficit/Hyperactivity
  Disorder (CHADD)
  http://www.chadd.org

- National Association of School Psychologists (NASP)
  http://nasponline.org

- National Institute of Mental Health (NIMH)
  http://www.nimh.nih.gov/health/topics/index.shtml

- National Resource Center on ADHD
  http://help4adhd.org

- Social Skills Training - Jed E. Baker, Ph.D.
  http://www.socialskillstrainingproject.com/books.html

- Understood: for learning and attention issues
  https://www.understood.org

References for Adults:

- Amen, Daniel G., M.D. *Healing ADD.* New York: Putnam, 2001.

- Ashley, Susan. *1000 Best Tips for ADHD: Expert Answers and Bright Advice to Help You and Your Child.* Illinois: Sourcebooks, 2012.

- Barkley, Russell A. *Taking Charge of ADHD, Third Edition: The Complete, Authoritative Guide for Parents.* New York: Guilford Press, 2013.

- Brown, Richard P., M.D. and Patricia L. Gerbarg, M.D. *Non-Drug Treatments for ADHD: New Options for Kids, Adults, and Clinicians.* New York: W. W. Norton & Company, 2012.

- Goldberg, Donna. *The Organized Student: Teaching Children the Skills for Success in School and Beyond.* New York: Touchstone, 2005.

- Hallowell, Edward M. M.D. and John J. Ratey M.D. *Delivered from Distraction: Getting the Most out of Life with Attention Deficit Disorder.* New York: Ballantine Books, 2006.

- Hallowell, Edward M. M.D. and John J. Ratey M.D. *Driven to Distraction: Recognizing and Coping with Attention Deficit Disorder from Childhood through Adulthood.* New York: Pantheon, 1996.

- Jensen, Peter S., M.D. *Making the System Work for Your Child with ADHD.* New York: Guilford Press, 2004.

- Jensen, Peter S., M.D. and James R. Cooper, M.D. *Attention Deficit Hyperactivity Disorder: State of the Science, Best Practices.* New Jersey: Civic Research Institute, 2002.

- Silver, Larry, M.D. *Dr. Larry Silver's Advice to Parents on ADHD.* New York: Three Rivers Press, 1999.

- Wilens, Timothy E., M.D. *Straight Talk About Psychiatric Medications for Kids.* New York: Guilford Press, 2002.

References for Kids (Grade Level):

- Dendy, Chris A. Ziegler and Alex Ziegler. *A Bird's-eye View of Life with ADD and ADHD: Advice from Survivors.* Alabama: Cherish the Children, 2003. **(Gr. 7+)**

- Fox, Janet S. *Get Organized Without Losing It (Laugh & Learn®).* Minnesota: Free Spirit Publishing, 2006. **(Gr. 6+)**

- Goldberg, Donna. *Teaching Children the Skills for Success in School and Beyond.* New York: Touchstone, 2005. **(Gr. K+)**

- Hallowell, Edward, M.D. *A Walk in the Rain with a Brain.* New York: HarperCollins, 2004. **(PreK-Gr. 6)**

- Kraus, Jeanne. *Cory Stories: A Kid's Book About Living With ADHD.* Washington, DC: Magination Pr, 2004. **(Gr. 3+)**

- Moss, Deborah. *Shelley, the Hyperactive Turtle.* Maryland: Woodbine House, 1989. **(PreK+)**

- Nadeau, Kathleen G. *Learning To Slow Down & Pay Attention: A Book for Kids About ADHD.* Washington, DC: Magination Pr, 2004. **(Gr. 4+)**

- Romain, Trevor. *How to Do Homework Without Throwing up (Laugh & Learn®).* Minnesota: Free Spirit Publishing, 2005. **(Gr. 3+)**

- Taylor, John F. *The Survival Guide for Kids with ADHD.* Minnesota: Free Spirit Publishing, 2013. **(Gr. 3-7)**

In-Depth 4114U Concepts:

Book Club Discussion Questions:

Written by: Colleen C. Ster

1. What game plan or strategies do you use to stay focused on your school work?

2. Do you feel that Jack appreciates his friendship with Smiley? If so, why?

3. If Jack doesn't like the lunch that his mom packs for him, what should he do to fix that problem?

4. What characteristics make somebody a bully at school? What techniques can you use to stop a bully?

5. How do Nate and Madeline get revenge on Lenny for treating their brother badly? Is revenge the best way to get even with someone that hurts you? What technique(s) do you like to use to resolve a conflict?

6. What are some ways you can make new friends at school if you have somebody like Lenny in a class, at your school, or on your sports team?

7. How do you stay organized with your school work?

8. How do you find a good book to read that you also find challenging?

9. How could talking to a parent or teacher be helpful if you feel you are struggling in school or having trouble focusing in the classroom or studying at home?

10. Do you have anyone who has stood up for you like Jack had Miss Robertson stand up for him? Have you ever stood up for someone in a tough situation?

Common Core State Standards
and AASL Standard Questions

Questions written by: Colleen Ster & Paula Yohe, M.L.S., M.Ed.

1. Why does Jack have so much trouble getting ready for school in the mornings? How do you know? What sentence(s) from the story support your answer?
   CCSS RL 5.1 AASL Standard(s) 1.1.6, 2.1.1

2. What is the theme of *BEEP!*? What details in the story help you determine the theme?
   CCSS RL 5.2 AASL Standard 1.1.6, 4.1.3

3. What are two major events in the story? How are they alike and different? How does each event contribute to the story?
   CCSS RL 5.3

4. On page 33, what is the meaning of "philosophized"? CCSS RL 5.4

5. How does the author use the way Jack responds to his situation to develop the theme of the story? CCSS RL 5.2
   AASL Standard 1.1.6, 4.1.3

6. How would the story be different if it had been told from Smiley's point of view rather than Jack's? CCSS RL 5.6

7. Read "What is ADD/ADHD" on pages 43-45. What are two main ideas of the article? Which key details support these main ideas? CCSS RI 5.2

8. Find digital and print information on ADHD. Summarize or paraphrase the information and include a list of resources. The information should be typed and a minimum of two pages. CCSS W 5.6 and W 5.7 AASL Standard(s) 1.1.1, 1.1.4, 1.1.6, 1.1.8, 1.1.9, 1.2.1, 1.2.2, 1.2.3, 1.3.4, 1.4.2, 1.4.4, 2.1.5, 3.1.3, 3.1.4, 3.2.3, 3.3.5, 4.2.3

9. Prepare a one minute multi-media presentation on ADHD to share with your class. CCSS SL 5.2 and SL 5.5 AASL Standard 1.1.6, 1.2.3, 2.1.6, 3.1.3, 3.1.4

10. On page 24, look at the word incessantly. Pronounce the word and read it in the sentence. Look at the definition of the word at the bottom of the page. Write another sentence using the word in context. SSCC RF 5.3 and 5.4

Chapter Books by Reflections Publishing:

BEEP!: Navigating Through ADHD
P: ISBN: 978-1-61660-013-6
Written & Illustrated by: Garrett Ritchie
4114U Illustrations: Julia Paul-Fisher

Crash: Overcoming Fear and Trauma
P: ISBN: 978-1-61660-006-8
Written by: Max Greenhalgh
Illustrated by: Jessa Weiner

Face 2 Face: Navigating Through Cyberbullying, Peer Abuse, & Bullying
P: ISBN: 978-1-61660-002-0
Written by: Caroline Ster
Illustrated by: Emily Jones

Falling to Pieces: Navigating The Transition to Middle School and Merging Friends
P: ISBN: 978-1-61660-007-5
Written by: Sarina Rogers
Illustrated by: Mia Rogers

Chapter Books by Reflections Publishing:

The Real Beauty: Navigating Through Divorce and Moving
P: ISBN: 978-1-61660-000-6
Written by: Kathryn Mohr
Illustrated by: Kiana Aryan

Scars: Navigating Through Peer Pressure & Consequences of Actions
P: ISBN: 978-1-61660-003-7
By Parent/Child Team: Dave, Julian, and Noelle Franco

Shining Through a Social Storm: Navigating Through Relational Aggression, Bullying, and Popularity
P: ISBN: 978-1-61660-004-4
Written by: Skylar Sorkin
Illustrated by: Sydney Green

Picture Books by Reflections Publishing:

Remind Me Again: Navigating Through the Loss of a Loved One
HC: ISBN: 978-1-61660-001-3
P: ISBN: 978-1-61660-010-5
Written by: The Ster Family
Illustrated by: Colleen C. Ster

A Mother's Love: Overcoming a Disability and Believing in Yourself
HC: ISBN: 978-1-61660-011-2
P: ISBN: 978-1-61660-008-2
Written by: Anthony Mazza
and Emmanuel Ofosu Yeboah

Remember Me When: Navigating Through Alzheimer's Disease
HC: ISBN: 978-1-61660-0012-9
P: ISBN: 978-1-61660-009-9
Written by: Isabelle Ster
Illustrated by: Emily Morgan

**Books Available through:
ReflectionsPublishing.com, amazon.com,
Follett Library Resources, Barnes and Noble,
Baker and Taylor, and Ingram.**